ISBN 0 361 05777 6
"Dangermouse" copyright © 1982 Cosgrove/Hall Productions Ltd
Text and illustrations copyright © 1983 Purnell Publishers Ltd
Published 1983 by Purnell Books, Paulton, Bristol BS18 5LQ
a member of the BPCC group of companies
Made and printed in Great Britain by A. Wheaton & Co. Ltd, Exeter

THE ADVENTURES OF DANGER MOUSE

Adapted by Greg Steddy
from the original TV scripts by Brian Trueman
Illustrated by Peter Campbell

Purnell

CONTENTS

DIE LAUGHING

At his secret hideout in London, the world's number one crimefighter was limbering up before breakfast with a few press-ups.

"6003, 6004, 6005," counted Penfold patiently. He was suddenly interrupted by the videophone.

"Oh 'eck, sir," he grumbled. "That'll be Colonel K."

"I'll see what he wants," said Dangermouse. "Just finish the last fifty for me will you, Penfold?"

The worried face of Colonel K appeared on the screen.

"Ah, there you are, DM," he began. "Something funny's happening."

"Funny ha ha or funny peculiar, Colonel?" asked Dangermouse.

"Bit of both," the Colonel

continued. "The world's top men are laughing themselves unconscious. There's panic abroad!"

"Best place for it!" chuckled Dangermouse. "What's the cause of it?"

"Well, at first it's a gas, then it changes into hundreds of tickling little beggars. Here, let me show you one . . ."

The screen changed to reveal a horrid little creature, laughing and chuckling.

"Boffins call it a Gigglococcus," explained the Colonel.

"Merry little microbe, isn't he?" muttered Dangermouse drily.

"Yes, but don't be fooled," said the Colonel gravely. "He's *deadly*!"

"Sounds like a pretty ticklish situation, Colonel."

"Worse than that, DM. We think the Prime Minister is next!"

"Good grief!" cried Dangermouse in alarm. "Don't worry, sir, we're on our way. Come on, Penfold!"

Seconds later they were driving at high speed across London. As they screeched to a halt outside the Prime Minister's secret hideout a strange machine emerged from the ground in front of them.

Inside the machine, the Master

of Evil, Baron Greenback, was plotting a dastardly scheme.

"OK, Stiletto," he hissed. "One blast of the gas through the grating and . . . Greenback rules."

Outside Dangermouse was eyeing the machine suspiciously.

"There can be only one person behind all this," he said grimly. "And I think it's about time we put a stop to it. Hang on, Penfold, we're going to ram the machine!"

"Curses! It's that interfering rodent!" screamed Greenback in a rage. "Quick! Fire the boosters!"

The machine shot into the air just as our heroes were about to ram it, and their car plunged headlong into the shaft beneath.

"Looks like we're going to get to the bottom of this quicker than we thought!" wailed Penfold miserably.

"Don't worry, Penfold," said Dangermouse, as he expertly landed the car at the foot of the shaft. "If this tunnel was made by that machine, it should lead back to their base. We'll stop those villains yet!"

They followed the tunnel for some while until they reached a fork.

"Funny place to leave cutlery," remarked Dangermouse. "Now I wonder which way we should go?"

"Back the way we came?" suggested Penfold hopefully.

A worm wearing a miner's helmet suddenly popped up in front of them.

"The tunnel you want is on the left," said the worm.

"Just a moment!" cried Dangermouse. "I know that voice! It's Agent 57!"

"I never could fool you, DM," laughed the worm, as they sped away.

"Agent 57 is our master of

disguise," explained Dangermouse. "Not even *he* knows what he really looks like!"

Just then, a huge jack-in-the-box sprang up underneath them and catapulted them through the roof of the tunnel. They were amazed to find themselves in a deserted Trafalgar Square.

"Crikey, DM! We're at the foot of Nelson's Column!" cried Penfold in confusion.

"Never mind his foot," said Dangermouse. "Look at his nose! There's something funny going on up there! Let's go and investigate!"

Inside the head of the statue, Greenback was rubbing his hands with glee (it's cheaper than handcream). His two henchmen, Stiletto and Leatherhead, stood on guard.

"Excellent, excellent!" gloated Greenback. "Soon my tickling task force can start a reign of terror that will bring the city to its knees! Then . . ."

"Sir," interrupted Stiletto urgently. "There's a car outside! It's coming up the column!"

"What?" roared Greenback.

"It's-a nearly here, Barone," cried Stiletto. "It's-a Dangermouse!"

"Don't worry," sniggered Greenback. "We'll give our guests something to laugh about. Get the gas cylinders ready!"

Not realising just how ticklish the situation was Dangermouse leapt from the car.

"Come on, Penfold!" he called impatiently. "We've got to find a way in."

"Hang on, chief," panted Penfold. "I've never climbed an admiral before!"

At that moment, a pigeon in policeman's uniform flapped up beside them.

"'ello, 'ello, 'ello. What's all this then?" inquired the pigeon suspiciously. "Is that your car parked on the admiral's epaulette?"

"Er, yes, constable," replied Dangermouse.

"*Sergeant*, if you don't mind, sir," said the pigeon wearily. "Now would you mind showing me your licence?"

His face dropped when he examined it, and he went bright

red — not a bad trick for a pigeon really.

"Er . . . oh, er . . . I *do* beg your pardon, sir. I had no idea . . ." he stammered. "If I can be of any help, Dangermouse, sir . . ."

Dangermouse brushed past, leaving the pigeon with his feathers in a fluster. He and Penfold made for a small door inside Nelson's head.

"Come on out!" cried Penfold nervously. "We know you're in there!"

"Who's there?" called Stiletto.

"Me!" replied Penfold.

"Me who?"

"Hey, chief, they've got a cat in there!" said Penfold in surprise.

"Well the cat's out of the bag!" cried Dangermouse. "Let's get them!"

They burst through the door and threw themselves to the ground as Stiletto and Leatherhead fired their gas guns. They missed our heroes and hit each other. Soon they were laughing and cackling uncontrollably.

Dangermouse leapt to his feet and found himself staring down the barrel of a huge gun.

"Good grief, Penfold!" he cried. "This must be Greenback's Gigglococcus Cannon!"

"Crumbs!" quavered Penfold.

"No, I think crunch would be better," chuckled Dangermouse, and he broke the cannon in half with a mighty karate chop.

"Look, sir!" whispered Penfold. "There's a rug sneaking out of the door!"

"No!" cried Dangermouse. "That's Greenback's pet — Nero! Quick, follow that caterpillar!" They chased Nero to the top of Nelson's hat, but suddenly Greenback appeared.

"There, there, Nero," he said

softly. "I won't let the nasty mouse get you."

"Your tickling days are over, you fiendish toad!" cried Dangermouse defiantly.

"I think not, fool!" sneered the toad. He drew back his coat to reveal a rocket pack underneath.

"Come, Nero, we must fly!" he gloated. "Farewell, White Wonder! I was made for higher things!" And with that he shot into the air and disappeared.

Back at Dangermouse's hideout, Colonel K was on the videophone.

"So Greenback had the last laugh, eh, DM?" he said.

"Afraid so, sir," replied Dangermouse. "4000 feet up, still climbing, and then the radar lost him!"

"Not to worry, DM," said the Colonel. "You saved the world at least — and you know what they say . . ."

"What's that, sir?"

"What goes up, must come down!"

"With a very big bump, I hope!" chuckled Penfold.

The BAD LUCK EYE of The LITTLE YELLOW GOD

In the quiet, relaxed atmosphere of his secret hideout, Dangermouse was enjoying a game of snooker. He was about to play a tricky shot on the black when the videophone buzzed loudly and ruined his concentration.

"Drat!" muttered Dangermouse. "That'll be Colonel K. Bang on cue!" He played the shot and the balls bounced all over the table until every one finally disappeared into the pockets.

"Crikey, chief!" cried Penfold. "Of all the luck!"

"Luck, Penfold?" snorted Dangermouse. "Luck doesn't come into it! Now I wonder what the Colonel wants?"

"Ah, there you are, DM," said Colonel K. "In the pink, I hope!"

"And the yellow, brown and green," muttered Penfold under his breath.

"Funny goings on, DM," continued the Colonel. "Do you believe in luck?"

"Good heavens, no, sir!" said Dangermouse.

"What?" protested Penfold. "After a shot like that?"

"That's enough, Penfold!" said Dangermouse sharply. "And put that lollipop away!"

"It's your old adversary, Baron Greenback," explained the Colonel. "Our chaps in Brazil say he's stolen an ancient charm from a remote mountain tribe. It's a strange emerald called the Bad Luck Eye of the Little Yellow God!"

"I don't like the sound of that, sir," said Penfold nervously.

"Worse still," said the Colonel, "is that people are being zonked by a mysterious green ray. It seems

to be coming from Australia, and anyone who cops it has absolutely ghastly bad luck!''

"Good grief!'' cried Dangermouse. "You think that Greenback is harnessing the power of the Bad Luck charm?"

"Exactly!'' said the Colonel gravely. "And heaven knows where he'll strike next!"

With a muffled cry, Colonel K suddenly disappeared under a large elephant that fell from above.

"Come on, Penfold!'' cried Dangermouse in alarm. "There's only one thing for it — to Australia!''

In less time than it takes to tell, our two heroes found themselves flying over unfamiliar countryside with a distinctly bad luck air about it.

"Look, Penfold!'' cried Dangermouse suddenly. "What's that sinister-looking building up ahead?"

A sign outside it read:
BARON GREENBACK'S BAD LUCK EMPORIUM — YOU ARE NOT WELCOME.

"We'll soon see about that!" said Dangermouse boldly, and they went inside. Sitting on top of a complex piece of machinery was a large green stone.

"The Bad Luck Eye!" whispered Dangermouse. "Now I wonder if . . ."

He pressed a button on the side of the machine and the emerald slid down towards them.

"Crumbs, chief!" cried Penfold in admiration. "Easy!"

"Yes," said Dangermouse thoughtfully. "Almost *too* easy. Why no guards? And where's Greenback?"

From a secret control room, the Master of Evil, Baron Greenback, was watching their progress intently.

"Ask a silly question, my interfering friend!" he hissed gleefully. "Now, Nero, let's sit back and watch the fun!"

"Cor, chief," cried Penfold. "That's great. The unluckiest thing in the world and you've just snatched it! You're a genius, DM, an absolute . . ."

His words tailed off as a black cloud formed mysteriously above their heads. Bolts of lightning suddenly rained down on them from all sides.

"This calls for drastic action!" cried Dangermouse.

"Waaagh!" yelped Penfold. "What do you mean, chief?"

"What I mean, Penfold," said Dangermouse, "is put that lollipop away — and *panic*!"

With a wild yell, they burst through the door and tripped down a long flight of steps, landing with a heavy thud against a tree at the foot of a cliff. A huge boulder fell with a crash on Dangermouse's head.

"Rock-a-bye-baby!" cackled Greenback triumphantly. "The green emerald brings disaster to anyone who carries it! Now, you mighty misfit, mind the minefields!"

"Come along, Penfold," said Dangermouse impatiently. "Just put that lollipop away and concentrate or you'll walk into a — waaagh!"

A bright flash and loud explosion cut him off in mid-sentence.

"Into a *what*, chief?" asked Penfold.

His words were drowned by another huge explosion.

"Into a minefield, Penfold!" said Dangermouse, trying hard to keep cool.

"Oh — a minefield," said Penfold casually. "A minefield? Waaagh!" and with that he rushed off, with mines exploding violently all around him.

"Stop, stop!" cried Dangermouse. "Don't run, walk — *carefully*! And for the last time, put that lollipop away!"

By walking very gently on tiptoe, they at last managed to get through the minefield. Ahead of them they saw a large perimeter fence with a sinister robot on patrol.

"Some kind of guard," whispered Dangermouse. "We'll sneak past it — just remember your jungle training!"

So saying, he tripped heavily over a hidden wire and set off a loud alarm bell.

"Crikey, sir," cried Penfold nervously. "Now you've done it!"

"Don't worry," said Dangermouse quickly. "Just keep still — robots can only detect movement!"

Instantly disproving this theory, the robot zoomed towards them, grabbed them in its strong mechanical arms and flung them bodily into a hole in the ground. When they came to, our heroes found that they were, yet again, prisoners of their arch-enemy, Baron Greenback.

"I've been keeping an eye on you two," hissed the villainous toad. "The Bad Luck Eye to be precise! But now I want it back — search them, Stiletto!"

"Si, Barone," said the crow, and he began to probe Penfold with a pair of long metal tongs. From his pocket he slowly pulled out Penfold's lollipop.

"Ah ha! Success!" he cackled.

"I have-a da Eye, Barone!"

"Stupid nerk!" protested Penfold. "That's not the . . ."

"Hush, Penfold!" interrupted Dangermouse sharply.

"Now, my friends," gloated the toad. "You're free to go. Your, er, transport awaits you. Best of bad luck on your trip!"

Our heroes were bundled helplessly into the barrel of a giant cannon and fired into space with a deafening roar.

"Well, at least we fooled that fat fiend," cried Dangermouse, as they flew through the air. "We've still got the emerald and he's got the lollipop!"

20

"But it was lime-flavoured!" whined Penfold miserably. "My favourite!"

"Bad for your teeth," said Dangermouse firmly. "Besides, we're in enough trouble as it is!"

Below them the South American continent slowly drifted into view.

"I say, Penfold," said Dangermouse. "That looks like Brazil. Isn't that where the Bad Luck Eye comes from?"

"Er, yes, chief," replied Penfold uneasily. "But why is it getting bigger?"

"Oh, that's because we're falling," said Dangermouse. "Falling? Waaagh!" With a

terrific splash they landed head first in the sea.

"Good job Colonel K fitted us out for every emergency!" spluttered Dangermouse. He pulled a cord and his suit inflated into a life raft, but at that moment a seagull swooped down and burst it with its beak.

"I think I've had enough of this emerald," muttered Dangermouse. "All we need now is . . ."

"Sharks!" yelled Penfold hysterically.

"Good grief!" cried Dangermouse. "Me and my big mouth — or rather theirs! We'll have to swim for it!"

With the great snapping fish in hot pursuit, our ill-fated heroes struck out desperately for land. Flinging themselves at last on to the shore, they plunged straight into dense jungle.

"Cor, isn't it dark?" said Penfold with a shiver. "Just you and me — and a giant gorilla! Waaagh!"

A giant gorilla bounded towards them, scrunched Dangermouse into a ball and bounced him across the clearing.

"I — I wouldn't do that if I were you," stammered Penfold bravely. "He's not going to be at all pleased."

"Why's that then, Jimmy?" asked the gorilla in a Scottish accent, as he casually flipped Dangermouse into the air.

"Because that's Dangermouse, that's why!"

"Dangermouse?" repeated the gorilla. "Dangermouse?"

"For heaven's sake!" persisted Penfold. "Why, he's the greatest . . . the best . . . the world's most famous detective and superhero!"

"Not *the* Dangermouse?" asked the gorilla in amazement. "Not the world's most famous detective and superhero?"

"The very same!"

"Och, that's terrible!" said the gorilla, apologising profusely. "I'm dreadful sorry, Jimmy. I didna mean to hurt ye." He unrolled Dangermouse and stood him shakily on the ground.

"Just a wee joke, ye know," laughed the gorilla nervously. "Here, Jimmy, have a wee banana!"

"No thank you, Jimmy," snapped Dangermouse crossly. "Lucky for him I didn't lose my temper," he muttered under his breath. "Come on, Penfold, let's take this emerald back where it belongs before we have any more bad luck!"

The gorilla gave a puzzled shrug,

finished the banana himself and flung the skin to the ground. Dangermouse and Penfold promptly slipped on it and landed with a thud on a teeming termites' nest.

"I just don't *believe* it!" exclaimed Dangermouse, as the termites picked them up and threw them over a cliff. "Ever get that feeling that it's not your day, Penfold?"

"Don't worry, chief," said Penfold brightly. "We're in luck. We're going to land in that lake!"

"Oh great!" said Dangermouse.

At that moment an elephant sucked up all the water from the lake and our heroes crashed heavily on to the dry lake bed.

"What happened to the water?" groaned Dangermouse.

The elephant replied by squirting it all over them.

"You great lump!" yelled Dangermouse furiously. "Just wait till I tell your mother. Elephants don't *do* that sort of thing!"

As he spoke another elephant swung across the clearing on a vine and flattened him. A hyena, laughing crazily, swung from the opposite direction and knocked him down again as he tried to get up. Dazed and bewildered, Dangermouse staggered to his feet as a large python dropped out of a tree and wrapped itself round him.

"Hey!" cried Dangermouse wearily. "Get this clown off me!" The snake slowly squeezed him until he went very purple in the face.

"Just stop that!" cried Dangermouse angrily. "Get off me, you overgrown inner-tube!"

"Sorry, old chap," chuckled the snake. "I'm just over*tired*, that's all!"

"Right! That does it!" snapped Dangermouse. "One silly joke too many! Here, laugh this one off!" He took the emerald out of his pocket and held it in front of the snake. With a cry of terror, the snake unwound itself and fled, spinning Dangermouse into the ground as he did so.

"Help me out of here, Penfold," he groaned. "We've got to get rid of this emerald before night falls."

Night fell with a heavy crash on Dangermouse's head.

"Oh no!" he cried in desperation. "I can't take any more, do you hear? I can't stand it!"

"What's that, chief?" said Penfold in surprise. "I didn't know *you* were frightened of the dark too!"

"It's not the dark, Penfold. It's the awful jokes! How do I get myself into these situations?"

"I dunno, chief. Just luck, I suppose!"

A terrible roaring sound behind them suddenly made them both spin round.

"What is it, chief?" cried Penfold in alarm.

"I don't know, Penfold," said Dangermouse firmly, "but I'm going to find out!"

He struck a match and the flickering light revealed a tiny mouse-like creature holding a stick with two large eyes painted on it.

"Roar! Roar!" roared the creature unconvincingly. "Er, would you believe — squeak?"

"Right!" said Dangermouse coldly. "I don't care who you are, I'm just sick to death of being blown up, shot down, shut in, kicked out and generally stamped on! I just want information — and fast!"

"Did I say I wouldn't talk?" stammered the creature. "So *ask* me!"

"Where's the village of the Bad Luck Tribe? I want to give their wretched charm back."

"Give it back?" cried the creature. "Are you crazy?"

"Where's — the — village?" said Dangermouse through clenched teeth.

"Over there," said the creature.

"But they won't like it, you'll see!" And with that it scuttled off into the bushes.

"Come on then, Penfold," said Dangermouse wearily. "Let's finish this business and get out of here!"

They set off through the trees and eventually came to a clearing. In the centre was a towering idol, around which were a number of fierce-looking natives dancing and singing.

"The Little Yellow God!" exclaimed Dangermouse with relief. "Penfold, we've done it!"

"Er, I think we should leave it alone," muttered Penfold nervously.

"Not until we've returned the emerald. Come on!"

Dangermouse walked boldly into the centre of the clearing.

"Hello there!" he called cheerfully. "Sorry to interrupt the fun, but I've brought your charm back!"

With a howl of terror the natives rushed at him and flung him bodily out of the village.

"They seem to be a bit confused," he said, dusting himself down, "but they're going to have it, *want* it or not!"

"Do be careful, chief!" cried Penfold anxiously.

Dangermouse stalked back towards the village, but was greeted by a hail of spears that thudded into the ground around him.

"Right, I'll show 'em!" he cried angrily. "I just happen to be able to control the beasts of the jungle!"

He gave a loud Tarzan call and a herd of elephants stampeded at them, trampling them into the ground.

"It's always worked before," he groaned. "It must be this cursed gem! I've *got* to get it back to them. I know — I'll go in disguise!"

Seconds later he was standing in front of Penfold, disguised as a bush.

"How's this, Penfold?"

"Er, I think you've got greenfly, chief!"

Dangermouse crept silently towards the village, but was immediately surrounded by the natives. With a fearsome cry, they smashed the bush to pieces with heavy clubs.

"OK, Penfold!" cried Dangermouse. "There's only one thing for it — a mass attack! Charge!"

tiresome, gentlemen!''

"Him have charm!" gabbled the native chief. "Him try give *us* charm. Him keep flippin' charm!"

"Quite so!" said Greenback with a sly grin. "Only *I* will take the charm and *you* will take Dangermouse."

"Fair swap!" agreed the chief. "Crocodile hungry!"

"Exactly!" gloated Greenback. "And I shall be left to rule the world! Quick, Stiletto, the protective clothing!"

"You want the charm, Baron?" said Dangermouse quickly. "It's yours!" He tossed the charm towards the toad, who instantly disappeared under a large walrus, that fell from above.

"Aaargh!" cried Greenback. "Not yet — I'm not ready! Here, Stiletto, *you* take it!"

"No, no, Barone!" screamed the crow, as a grand piano fell on his head. The gem flew into the chief's hands. He looked at it nervously for a couple of seconds, then disappeared howling under a great pile of flying objects.

"Oh, bad luck, old bean!" chuckled the toad. His laughter died in his throat as the gem flew into the air and landed in his mouth.

"Oh no! Aaargh!" he yelled, as

Dragging a reluctant Penfold with him, he raced into the village and landed with a thump against a very familiar figure.

"So, Dangermouse," hissed a malevolent voice. "We meet again!"

"Greenback!" cried Dangermouse. "I might have known!"

"What bad luck!" sneered the toad. "I'm sorry if this meddlesome mouse is being a herd of buffalo trampled over him. He fled screaming into the jungle, being hit by great boulders, bolts of lightning and a vast assortment of nasty things.

". . . and that's the last we saw of him," said Penfold, as he reported the story much later to Colonel K. "And good riddance too, I say."

"Quite right, Penfold," agreed the Colonel. "By the way, how's Dangermouse?" asked the Colonel.

"Oh, he's as right as ninepence, sir," said Penfold. "It's just left him a bit superstitious, that's all."

"Superstitious?" queried the Colonel.

"Yes, sir," continued Penfold. "He insists on carrying a rabbit's foot for luck."

Just then Dangermouse appeared dragging a large struggling rabbit.

"The only thing is," chuckled Penfold, "the rabbit doesn't want to give it up!"

The FOUR TASKS of DANGERMOUSE

In his five-bedroomed detached pillar box in Mayfair, Dangermouse was pacing anxiously to and fro. That very morning, disaster had struck. His faithful assistant, Penfold, had been kidnapped on his way back from the sweetshop by his arch-enemy, Baron Greenback. The videophone suddenly bleeped loudly and Colonel K appeared.

"I'm here, sir," said Dangermouse quickly. "Is there any news?"

"It's Greenback!" replied the Colonel.

"No, sir, it's you!"

"I mean it's Greenback on the videophone — he wants to talk to you!"

"The unprincipled villain!" muttered Dangermouse angrily. "Put him on!"

The evil face of Greenback appeared on the screen.

"Ah, Dangermouse," he sneered. "It's Penfold."

"No, Baron, it's you!" cried Dangermouse.

"I mean I've *got* Penfold!"

"You fiend!" said Dangermouse through clenched teeth. "What have you done with him?"

"Oh, he's quite safe, I assure

31

you. See for yourself!''

The screen changed to Penfold looking very sorry for himself in a dingy little cell.

''Penfold, are you all right?'' asked Dangermouse with concern.

''I am being treated well,'' replied Penfold flatly. ''The frost in my cell is very pretty, I'm not hungry anyway and er, er . . .''

''The beetles!'' prompted Greenback.

''Oh yes,'' said Penfold. ''And the beetles are awfully friendly!''

''See!'' cackled Greenback. ''He loves it!''

''You green devil!'' cried Dangermouse angrily. ''What is it you want from me?''

''Only your help, my friend,'' said Greenback with a sly grin. ''There is an ancient spell for creating an invincible monster and I would *so* like to try the recipe, but alas, the ingredients are a little hard to come by . . .''

''And I shall stop you *ever* getting them!'' cried Dangermouse.

''I think not!'' hissed Greenback. ''Because if you do . . .''

His voice tailed off and Penfold appeared on the screen, suspended over a large box of dynamite. There was nothing Dangermouse

could do.

''OK, Baron,'' he sighed. ''What do you want?''

''I *knew* you'd want to help!'' gloated the toad. ''Now then, all I need is a twig from a witch's broom, four hairs from a yeti, a piece of the dreaded Fog Monster of Old London Town, and two feathers from a vampire duck! Get them and Penfold lives. But should you fail — boom!'' He cackled.

''OK, you scoundrel,'' said

Dangermouse grimly. "You win this time — but I'll be back!"

So with a heavy heart and an empty passenger seat, Dangermouse set off for the Himalayas on the first of his quests — to take four hairs from a yeti!

He soon became aware of a low rumbling in the distance.

"This is a fine time to fly into a thunderstorm," he thought, as he swooped in over a low peak. To his delight he saw the huge figure of a sleeping yeti lying on the mountainside, snoring loudly. He landed quickly and crept towards the enormous creature, armed with a large pair of scissors, but just then the yeti breathed out with such force that Dangermouse was blown into a tree. He picked himself up determinedly, but was again blown back against the tree, which broke and landed on his head with a sharp crack.

"I think I'd better try another

approach!'' he groaned, rubbing his head painfully.

He climbed a low cliff above the yeti and with an evil grin pushed a large rock on to his sleeping foe below. With a loud snore, the yeti blew the rock back into the air. It landed with a dull thud on Dangermouse.

''I suppose you think that's funny!'' An angry muffled voice came from under the rock.

He heaved the heavy rock away and muttered, ''I'll get you this time!'' as he edged his way along the branch of a tree above the yeti's head and reached down tentatively with the scissors. At that moment, the yeti awoke with a start and, spotting an apple above him, bent the branch towards him. He grabbed the apple and let go of

the branch, sending Dangermouse flying into the air. With that he shuffled off into his cave.

Dangermouse crashed heavily into a thicket and staggered slowly back towards the cave, where a strange sight met his eyes. The yeti was standing in front of a mirror, combing out his long hair and humming a tune. Pulling the loose hairs out of the comb, he dropped them absent-mindedly all over Dangermouse.

"Talk about overdoing it!" he coughed. "I must have got *forty* hairs here! Now — what's next? Good grief! A piece of the dreaded Fog Monster of Old London Town! Oh well, for Penfold's sake — to London!"

Thick fog swirled around Dangermouse as he crept warily

through the streets of Whitechapel. Groping his way round a gloomy corner, he bumped suddenly into something large and solid.

"Oh, I beg your pardon," he said politely, then froze as he realised he was in the presence of none other than — the dreaded Fog Monster of Old London Town!

"Er, how do you do?" he stammered. "I wonder if I might just take this small piece here?" He made a grab at the monster, but it howled with pain and shot into the air. Transforming itself into a huge ball, it bounced back on Dangermouse and knocked him flat.

"Oh come on, be reasonable!" gasped Dangermouse. "Just a small piece!"

The monster descended once more and with a childish giggle changed Dangermouse into a clown.

"Right, that does it!" cried Dangermouse angrily, and leapt at the monster with a long piece of rope. He soon had it bound securely, but it immediately turned back into a cloud and the rope fell harmlessly to the ground. At that moment the phone rang.

"That might be Colonel K," said Dangermouse hopefully.

"He'll know what to do!"

He picked up the phone, but the monster, assuming the shape of a fist, shot out of the receiver and punched Dangermouse on the nose. While he was still lying dizzily on the floor, the monster came back as a large bucket and poured mud all over him.

"I've just about reached breaking point!" snapped Dangermouse. "Now look — I'll swap you — what do you fancy? Power? Riches! Fast cars?"

The monster gave a silly laugh and formed the word *chocolate* from the fog.

"Chocolate, eh?" said Dangermouse with relief. "Here, try this!"

The monster ate the chocolate bar greedily.

"How about two bars a day for ever?" asked Dangermouse.

The monster let out a cry of delight and a small piece of itself broke away and drifted into Dangermouse's hands.

". . . so that's two out of four, Colonel," said Dangermouse, as he reported his progress so far. "Half way to Penfold's freedom!"

The screen cut to a picture of Greenback, rubbing his hands in anticipation.

"Very good, my mousey friend!" he hissed. "Now off you trot and find Uncle Greenback two nice feathers from a vampire duck!"

Within hours our intrepid hero had ventured boldly into the depths of darkest Transylvania.

"Vampire ducks? Huh!" he muttered to himself. "How can I get two feathers from something that doesn't exist? Vampire ducks indeed!"

With a puff of smoke a vampire duck suddenly appeared.

"Who calls so loud?" it cried.

"Good grief!" exclaimed Dangermouse. "I thought you were a myth!"

"Sir!" replied the duck arrogantly. "I am not even a *mythter* — I am a Count!"

"A Count!" gasped Dangermouse. "Not . . ."

"Yes, yes," interrupted the duck impatiently. "*The* Count — Count Duckula — at your service. What is't you seek?"

"Well, er, as a matter of fact," stammered Dangermouse. "A — a couple of your feathers actually!"

"Feathers, varlet?" shrieked the Count. "Two of my *feathers*? Never! I am a duck, not a duster. I am Count Duckula of Transylvania!"

"But, Count, it's vital!" cried Dangermouse anxiously. "My assistant will die if I don't get them! Ask me *anything* in exchange. Anything you really want!"

"Anything?" echoed the Count.

"Anything!"

"Could you get me on television?"

"On television?" asked Dangermouse in surprise. "Doing what?"

"Anything!" cried the Count. "Er, magic — how about that?"

"Well, I don't know," mused Dangermouse.

"You will be astounded!" persisted the Count. "I will produce, not rabbits out of hats, but hats out of rabbits! Behold!"

"Well, er . . ." began Dangermouse doubtfully.

"There is yet more, much more!" cried the Count. "Come, saw me in half, my friend!"

He rushed over and lay in a coffin with his head sticking out of the end. With a puzzled look on his face, Dangermouse sawed the Count in half from top to bottom.

"Is that what you wanted?" he asked, shaking his head.

"Er, not entirely," replied the Count slowly. "No matter!" With a puff of smoke, he became his original self.

"Do you like bats?" he asked suddenly. "Then behold!"

A flock of bats appeared above them, followed by a cricket bat floating in the air.

"A plague on it!" cried the Count, stamping his foot. "False erroneous bat! Begone! Nay, but forget the conjuror's tricks —

more can I do! Behold — Count Duckula now plays Hamlet!"

In a flash he was dressed as Hamlet, holding a skull.

"Alas, poor Yorick!" he bellowed. "I knew him, Horatio!"

"Er, look, Count," interrupted Dangermouse nervously. "I don't know how to say this but, er, I don't think television is quite ready for you yet!"

"Then, sir," replied the Count pompously, "I am not ready to give you my feathers! Farewell!"

"Oh, it's like that, is it?" muttered Dangermouse. "Right, Mr. Showbiz, this will put you among the stars!"

He tossed a harmonica at the Count, who grabbed it eagerly.

"A harmonica!" he exclaimed. "Right, world — just listen to this!" he cried, changing instantly into a striped blazer and straw hat. As he began to play a tune there was a loud bang and the harmonica blew up in his face and the Count dropped to the ground in a cloud of black smoke. Dangermouse rushed over and snatched two feathers from his smoking rump.

"Thanks, Count!" he chuckled as he sped off. "That last act of yours went like a bomb! Now for the final ingredient — a twig from a witch's broom!"

After much searching Dangermouse located a remote cottage where, it was rumoured, a wicked witch lived. He spotted a note on the table which read: NO MILK TODAY — OFF FOR A SHORT SPELL — BACK SATURDAY —

THE WICKED WITCH.

"Now there's a stroke of luck!" thought Dangermouse. "If she's away till Saturday, I'll just help myself to a bit of her broom!"

But as he went to grab it, it darted off round the room and evaded all attempts to catch it.

"Playing hard to get, eh?" snarled Dangermouse. "OK, you yardbrush, let's see you get out of this!"

He threw a lasso expertly round the broom, but it set off again dragging Dangermouse with it.

"Come back here!" gasped Dangermouse. "You won't feel a thing, honest!"

The broom stopped suddenly and Dangermouse crashed heavily into it.

"Aha!" he cried in triumph. "Now I've got you! This won't hurt."

He broke off a twig, but the twig dragged him off round the room and up the chimney.

"OK, you little devil!" cried Dangermouse, pulling out a gun. "Hold it right there!"

The magic twig turned the gun into a flower and Dangermouse threw it down in disgust.

"All right," he snapped. "Try this for size!"

He grabbed the twig and tied it to a large weight. The twig lifted it effortlessly into the air and dropped it on Dangermouse's head, driving him into the ground.

"Sorry, Penfold," he groaned. "I think I've met my match this time!"

"Eh? What was that, boyo?" said the twig suddenly. "Penfold, did you say? Not the Penfold with an auntie in Abergavenny?"

"Well, I think he *does* have a Welsh auntie," said Dangermouse with surprise.

"Aw, why ever didn't you say

so?'' said the twig apologetically. "Known his family since they were nippers. Here, boyo, cop hold!'' And with that he pulled Dangermouse out of the ground.

"What's goin' on then?'' continued the twig. "Is Penfold in danger?''

"He's been kidnapped by Baron Greenback,'' explained Dangermouse. "He's found an ancient spell to create a monster and I have to get him the ingredients — or Penfold's for it!''

"What ingredients are those then, boyo?'' asked the twig.

"Well, there's a piece of the dreaded Fog Monster . . .''

"So he can be any shape. Yes . . .''

"And four hairs from a yeti . . .''

"That's for strength!''

"Two feathers from a vampire duck . . .''

"That's so he'll never die.''

"And *you*!'' concluded Dangermouse.

"Ah, that's for intelligence, naturally!'' chuckled the twig.

"Well he's had it, see! I'll teach him to kidnap my great aunt's second cousin! Now here's what we do . . ."

Meanwhile in Greenback's lair, Penfold was chained miserably above a pit of snapping crocodiles.

"It won't be long now!" cackled the evil toad. "Soon I will rule the world!"

"Oh no you won't!" said Penfold defiantly. "Dangermouse won't let you, so there!"

"Dangermouse?" sneered Greenback. "Do you think I fear that wretched rodent? Eh, Stiletto?"

"Afraid of-a da mouse?" laughed the crow. "Very good, Barone! Hey, here is-a Dangermouse!"

"What?" cried the toad in

43

alarm. "Quickly!" He pressed a button and an armoured wall rose up around them.

"Right!" he stammered. "Let in the p-p-pathetic creature!"

The door opened and Dangermouse slowly entered.

"Now don't do anything silly," said the toad, panicking slightly. "Or Penfold drops in for lunch!" OK, Stiletto, make sure he can't escape!"

Dangermouse was soon tied, chained and caged in the centre of the room. Only then would Greenback lower the armoured wall.

"Poor wee cowering timorous beastie!" gloated the toad. "If only you had my courage! Now for the magic ingredients!" He grabbed them and mixed them,

following the spell. "What's this? They don't work!"

"Oh but they do, Mr. Greenback," said a deep voice. "When you actually *have* them!"

With that, the figure of Dangermouse turned into a cloud and floated out of the cage.

"We've been cheated!" raged Greenback. "That's not Dangermouse — it's the magic monster! Then Penfold dies!"

He pressed a button and Penfold was suddenly released over the crocodile pit, but quick as a flash the monster extended a long hand and whisked him to safety.

"Tough luck, Baron, boyo," chuckled the monster. "You should have known there was a catch in it!"

He turned swiftly on the villains and soon they were bound hand and foot. At that moment, Dangermouse walked in and Penfold leapt into his arms with a cry of joy.

"I say, steady on, Penfold!" said Dangermouse, feeling a trifle embarrassed. "We *are* British, don't forget!"

"Oh, sorry, chief!" cried Penfold happily. "It's just so good to see you!"

"I know, Penfold, I know!" said Dangermouse modestly.

"Here we are, boyos!" interrupted the monster cheerfully. "Gift-wrapped villains!"

"Great stuff!" said Dangermouse, nodding with approval. "But what are we going to *do* with them?"

"Yes, I've been thinkin' about that," said the monster. "Thought they might fancy a little cruise!"

"A cruise?" protested Penfold.

"Yes, yes," continued the monster. "Just to the Milky Way and back. Shouldn't take more than a couple o' thousand years?"

"But how do we get them there?" asked Dangermouse.

"With me, boyo, with me?" beamed the monster. "I'm a bit bored with flittin' over rooftops with that old witch, so I'm not goin' back to bein' a broom. I'm goin' to be a spaceship!"

So saying, the monster wrapped himself around Greenback and his helpless accomplices, turned himself into a spaceship and blasted off into space.

". . . and that's the last we saw of them, Colonel!" said Dangermouse, reporting the strange tale to Colonel K.

"Jolly good show too, DM!" said the Colonel. "And welcome back, Penfold, old boot! Good to have you around. Fit for another job then, eh?"

"I should say so, sir!" said Penfold eagerly. "I seem to have done nothing but hang about just lately!"

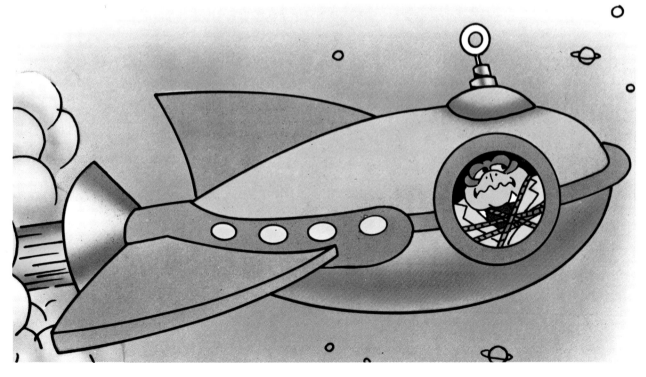

The DREAM MACHINE

Dangermouse and Penfold awoke with a start. The videophone was bleeping loudly and Colonel K appeared on the screen.

"Ah, Dangermouse," he said. "Ready to spring to the defence of the weak and helpless?"

"As ever, Colonel," replied Dangermouse. "What's up?"

"Well," continued the Colonel. "A strange sort of cloud's been floating about over London."

"A cloud, sir?" interrupted Dangermouse. "What sort of cloud?"

"Well, it's got odd flashing lights popping about inside it and . . ." The Colonel's words died away as a cloud with odd flashing lights popping about inside it descended over him. When it cleared, all that remained was the Colonel's empty chair.

"Crikey, sir!" cried Penfold in alarm. "He's turned into a chair!"

"No, Penfold," said Dangermouse grimly. "He's been cloudnapped!"

"But how, sir?" asked Penfold.

"I haven't the foggiest idea!" said Dangermouse. "We know the

Colonel's gone — now all we need to find out is how, why and with whom — and we've cracked it! Come on!''

Within seconds they were in hot pursuit of the sinister cloud, little knowing that *it* would find *them*.

''Good grief, Penfold!'' cried Dangermouse suddenly. ''We've just been engulfed by an enormous great cloud!''

''Thank goodness for that!'' said Penfold with relief. ''I thought my glasses had steamed up!''

''I'd guess it was a cumulo-nimbus,'' mused Dangermouse.

''Didn't he discover America?'' asked Penfold.

''*Do* be serious, Penfold,'' said Dangermouse. ''There appears to be nothing in this cloud!''

''Wrong!'' cackled a very familiar voice. ''There's me!''

The disembodied head of their arch-enemy, Baron Greenback, suddenly floated before their eyes.

''Welcome to my dream machine, gentlemen!'' sniggered the toad. ''It will make all your favourite nightmares come true!''

''You pea-green devil!'' shouted Dangermouse, angrily.

''Oh, how ungrateful!'' said Greenback with a leer. ''I only made it to help you out!''

''Help us out?'' said Penfold suspiciously.

''Help you out of your minds!'' cried the toad, laughing hysterically. ''Inside my dream machine, only the impossible is possible. Now, farewell — and unpleasant dreams!''

His head disappeared for a second, then returned.

''Oh, I nearly forgot,'' he sniggered. ''Don't, whatever you do, say — rock!''

''Rock?'' echoed Penfold. A large rock dropped from nowhere on to Dangermouse's head.

''I don't get it, chief,'' said Penfold, with a puzzled frown.

"All I said was rock!" Dangermouse disappeared under another large rock.

"Waaagh!" yelled Dangermouse. "Look, Penfold, just don't say R-O-C-K!"

"Why not?" asked Penfold blankly.

"The thing is, Penfold," said Dangermouse, rubbing his head, "that whenever you mention 'you know what' they appear. So just be careful!"

"OK, DM," said Penfold, "I'll watch it!" A huge watch swung silently through the air. Dangermouse jumped to one side — but too late! He was knocked to the ground.

"My timing seems to have deserted me, Penfold," he groaned. "Come on, we've got to find a way out of here."

"Hang on, sir," said Penfold. "My feet are like lead!"

A pair of heavy lead boots

appeared on his feet and he
crashed through the floor with a
wild yell.

"Oh, really, Penfold," said
Dangermouse. "Can't you be more
careful. We're getting nowhere
fast!"

He was right of course. They
stumbled along for what seemed
ages through Greenback's
Dungeon of Dreams. There was no
sign of Colonel K and worse still
no sign of a way out. Eventually,
Dangermouse thought he could see
a door ahead of them.

"Hello, what's that?" he
remarked. "Looks like a way
out!"

"Steady on, chief," said
Penfold nervously. "You don't
think it could be a, well you know,
a trap? Waaagh!"

A trap-door opened beneath him
and he fell through with a crash.

"I'm falling, sir!" he yelled.

Dangermouse thought quickly.

"OK, Penfold," he shouted.
"What do you do when you're
frightened?"

"I scream!" screamed Penfold.

With a huge splash he landed in
a giant ice-cream sundae. Peering
over the edge of the glass, he was
terrified to see a large pair of eyes
staring at him in the dark.

"W-w-what's that?" he stammered. "Are you a spider?"

"Maybe!" said a voice.

"Er, well, are you a gorilla?" he asked.

"Could be!" said the voice.

"Are you a pterodactyl then?"

"I might be!"

"Are you a green monster?"

"No!"

"Oh good," said Penfold with relief.

"I'm a red monster!" laughed the voice.

"Waaagh! That's not so good!" cried Penfold shakily. "Er, how big are you?"

"Oh, I'm very big," replied the voice. "How big are you?"

"Ah, well," said Penfold, trying to sound brave. "I'm, er, much bigger than that!"

"You don't *sound* very big," said the voice.

"Er, well, I'm lying down!" said Penfold boldly. "Now, for the last time, what *are* you?"

"I'm a Lesser-spotted Penfold-eater!" growled the voice.

"Waaagh! Help!" cried Penfold, starting to panic. "Oh, I wish it wasn't so dark!"

In a flash it was suddenly light again and Penfold found himself face to face with a tiny little creature holding two long sticks with large cut-out eyes on the ends. It took one look at Penfold and scooted off in terror.

Penfold looked around him and wondered where on earth he was.

"If only I could find Dangermouse," he muttered to himself. "I feel such a weed on my own!"

"Up here, Penfold!" called a familiar voice.

Penfold looked up and saw

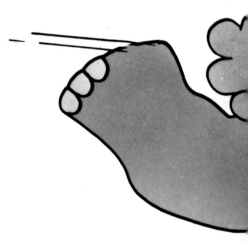

Dangermouse's head at the top of a tall plant.

"Crikey, DM!" he cried in surprise. "I wish you were back to normal!"

With that, the plant vanished and Dangermouse fell to earth with a bump.

"Thank you, Penfold!" said Dangermouse painfully. "It looks as though we could be in here for quite a while!"

"Hey, what's that noise?"

interrupted Penfold suddenly.

"I didn't hear anything," replied Dangermouse. "What did it sound like?"

"Well," began Penfold. "It's hard to describe. It's a bit like, well, like a ballet-dancing elephant on a skateboard?"

"Good old Penfold!" laughed Dangermouse. "It's good to keep up a sense of humour at a time like this."

A ballet-dancing elephant on a skateboard flashed by and waved at them cheerily.

"Just a minute!" cried Dangermouse. "I've got it! It's *you,* Penfold! Greenback has programmed his machine to respond to anything you say!"

"Crikey, chief!" said Penfold, feeling very flattered. "Anything I say — wow?"

"Stop it, Penfold!" said Dangermouse sharply. "Now the dream machine is inside a cloud, right? So all we need to do is think up some bad weather and shift it with a good blow!"

"Righto then, chief!" said Penfold. "Watch this!"

It started to snow heavily.

"No, no, Penfold!" cried Dangermouse. "I said blow, not snow!"

"But I *like* snow," whined

Penfold. "You can make snowmen, and go skiing and sledging, and have super fights with snowb . . . Waaagh!" His words were cut short by a huge snowball that flattened him.

"Serves you right, Penfold!" scolded Dangermouse. "Anyway, I've had a better idea. We'll blow the cloud away with a big fan!"

"A big fan?" echoed Penfold.

A large shaggy dog ran towards them with a sign round its neck saying 'DM IS ACE'.

"Honestly, Penfold!" groaned Dangermouse. "Not that sort of fan! Try again."

A giant wind fan appeared before them. Dangermouse switched it on and it blew the cloud away, revealing a strange flying machine.

"OK, Greenback!" he cried. "The game's up! I've come to bring you to justice!"

"Indeed!" hissed Greenback defiantly. "You and whose army?"

"Funny you should say that, Baron," said Dangermouse. "Perhaps you'd care to take a look outside!"

The evil toad was horrified to see that he was surrounded by a

thousand Dangermice.

"I'm afraid your dream machine has backfired, Baron!" laughed Dangermouse. "Penfold said 'Dangermouse' a thousand times!"

"Curse you, Dangermouse, er, mice!" raged the toad, as the army of mice closed in . . .

Some time later, Colonel K was being filled in on the story.

"So you see, sir," said Dangermouse. "Faced with a thousand Dangermice, he gave in, and after we dropped you off we just turned him loose."

"What?" cried the Colonel in disbelief. "You mean the blighter's still floating about in that infernal machine?"

"Oh yes, sir," replied Dangermouse. "But we're keeping an eye on him!"

"We?" asked the Colonel.

"The other thousand mes, sir," laughed Dangermouse.

"Oh, that's all right then," said the Colonel, with relief. "Tell you what, though. I hope they're not all going to ask for a week's wages!"

"We wouldn't dream of it, Colonel!" chuckled Dangermouse.

A MONUMENTAL ROBBERY

Dangermouse and Penfold were having a well-earned rest, totally unaware of the dastardly crimes that were striking at the heart of every capital city in the world. Their peace was shattered as the videoscreen crackled into life. It was Colonel K.

"Hello, Colonel," said Dangermouse cheerfully. "Anything wrong?"

"Wrong, DM?" blared the Colonel. "A disaster! Half the world's historic buildings have vanished!"

"Good grief!" exclaimed Dangermouse incredulously. "Vanished?"

"That's what I said," continued the Colonel. "The Tower of London, the Kremlin, the Eiffel Tower — all gone! And we've just heard that the Empire State

Building's disappeared as well!''

"Say no more, sir!'' cried Dangermouse. "We're on our way!''

And with that, he shot down the lift into his car, dragging a reluctant Penfold with him.

Soon they were speeding away high over the rooftops.

"I say, Penfold, is that Shepherd's Bush down there?'' inquired Dangermouse.

"Looks like it, sir,'' said Penfold.

"Oh good,'' said Dangermouse. "Then we're right on course for America!''

"Why America, sir?'' Penfold looked blank.

"That's where the last building disappeared from, of course,'' said Dangermouse. "And I hope that's where we'll pick up the trail of the villains!''

After a while they passed the familiar sight of the Statue of Liberty, but they headed on towards the desert.

"Crumbs, sir,'' cried Penfold suddenly. "We must be lost! Look down there — it's the Tower of London!''

"No, Penfold,'' said Dangermouse. "It's the Tower that's lost! Better go down and take a look!''

They had barely landed when a strange-looking cowboy galloped up and pulled his horse to a violent halt beside them.

"I say, boy,'' he cried to Dangermouse. "What you sellin'? Love the suit, hate the mask!''

Dangermouse looked at him in amazement.

"Well I'll be hornswaggled!'' continued the cowboy. "You must be makin' a picture!''

"Pleased to meet you, Mr. — er, Hornswaggled," said Dangermouse politely.

"McGraw's the name, boy," corrected the cowboy. "Texas Jack McGraw — TJ to my friends!"

"Er, well, actually," began Dangermouse, more confused than ever, "we were just admiring this magnificent edifice of yours."

"Edifice?" said Texas Jack with a puzzled frown. "I thought he invented the gramophone. Oh — you mean this little ol' country house of mine. I just knew it was right for my million-acre backyard as soon as that there fella made it grow!"

"Which fellow was that, TJ?" asked Dangermouse, now totally lost.

"Why, a little round green fella," replied Texas Jack. "Said it was a genuine antickity!"

"Oh, it's that all right, TJ," said Dangermouse. "It's the Tower of London!"

"Great leapin' hornytoads!" exclaimed Texas Jack. "And to think I gave him my pearl-handled colt 45s *and* my genuine autograph of John Wayne for it! I guess you'd better take it back, little buddy!"

"I'm afraid so, TJ," said Dangermouse. "The fact is your

green friend was none other than Baron Silas Greenback, the world's most villainous toad!"

"Well from now on, I'm gunnin' for him!" cried Texas Jack. "Him and his sidekicks went that-a-way. I'm goin' back for Old Betsy!"

"This is no job for a woman!" protested Penfold.

"I love it!" laughed Texas Jack. "Hey, little fella, you've got about as much grip as a raccoon in a

wretched rodent interfering?''

Nero squeaked excitedly in his ear.

"Hmm," mused the toad. "You could be right, my little pet. Stiletto, we'll try the cannon!"

A long barrel slid from the machine and fired a large shell towards Dangermouse and Penfold.

"Crikey, sir!" exclaimed Penfold. "I don't think we're welcome here. Quick, start the car!"

"Fear not, little friend," said Dangermouse boldly. "Remember, a hero's car always starts in the nick of time . . . well, nearly always! Waaaghh!"

The shell exploded above them, covering them with a cloud of gas. Within seconds they had shrunk to a miniscule size.

When the air cleared they found themselves helplessly trapped in a glass jar on Greenback's desk.

"My, my, Dangermouse, you *have* come down in the world!" cackled Greenback wickedly. "Let me show you my latest secret weapon."

He pressed a button and Nelson's Column, the Sphinx and Hollywood Bowl materialised in a cloud of gas before them. He pressed another and the buildings

barrel of oil! Old Betsy's my twelve-bore shotgun!''

Meanwhile, the evil toad had been putting his masterplan into action. All the stolen buildings were arranged into a great travelling city on a huge wheeled machine. From the control room at the heart of this deadly device, he was watching the progress of our heroes with increasing rage.

"Curses!" he screamed. "Can't I do anything without that

shrank back to tiny dots.

"Simple, isn't it?" gloated the toad. "When you're a genius!"

He laughed a mad laugh, but a cry of alarm from Stiletto cut him short.

"Hey, Barone, I gotta da problem!"

A tribe of fearsome-looking Red Indians suddenly burst in and dragged Greenback outside.

"Take your hands off me!" he squealed, as he was bundled into a waiting Chevrolet car. "Stiletto! Help!"

"Sorry, Barone!" said the crow, struggling to free himself. "I'm a bit tied up at da moment!"

With that, the car roared away in a cloud of dust.

"Crumbs, chief!" muttered Penfold uneasily. "Now we're in a jam!"

"Well, we're certainly in a jar!" concluded Dangermouse. "We've got to find a way to get out."

Their hopes were shrinking fast when the sound of galloping hooves came to their ears and a familiar voice cried out:

"OK, you green horny toad, I double dare you to come out of there!"

"It's Jack!" exclaimed Penfold, breathing a sigh of relief. "Get us out of here!"

"My, my, little buddy!" chuckled Jack, as he saw their plight. "You really *are* little!"

"Quick, Jack, press that button!" cried Dangermouse.

With a flash and a puff of smoke, our hapless heroes were returned to their normal height.

"That was Greenback's fiendish weapon," explained Dangermouse. "But he's given us the slip, I'm afraid. All we heard was a car!"

"A car!" cried Jack. "By golly, Chevvy tracks! That means the Flatfeet have got 'em! And good riddance, I say!"

"No, Jack," said Dangermouse. "We must bring them to justice. See if you can spot them for me, will you, Penfold?"

He pressed the button and with a roar Nelson's Column grew rapidly under Penfold's feet.

"Waaagh! Get me down!" wailed Penfold, clinging desperately to the Admiral's nose. "They're over there, but just get me down!"

Dangermouse operated the machine once more and Penfold landed with a bump.

"Now all we need is a way to rescue them," said Dangermouse.

"What you need," suggested Jack, "is the good ol' US Cavalry, by gosh!"

"Good idea!" cried Dangermouse. "Come on!"

In the Indian village, Greenback and his henchmen were the centre of attention. To be precise, they were tied to totem poles while the Indians danced menacingly around them.

"Look, can't we discuss this?" spluttered Greenback. "Don't you realise I'm the world's most powerful toad?"

"Fat frog speak with forked tongue!" snarled the chief contemptuously.

"Hey, Barone," whispered Stiletto. "What we need is the cavalry to rescue us!"

"Hah! Me plenty scared!" laughed the chief sarcastically. "Me heap afraid of General Custard!"

At that moment a trumpet fanfare sounded.

"The cavalry!" screamed the Indians, scattering in all directions.

Tossing their trumpets aside, Texas Jack, Dangermouse and Penfold galloped at full pelt into the Indian camp.

"Cavalry, indeed!" snorted Greenback in disgust.

"Allow us to offer you a lift, Baron," cried Dangermouse. "To jail!"

"Thanks for everything, Jack!" called Penfold. "So long, pardner!"

Back in London, our heroes were reporting the strange tale to Colonel K.

". . . and you're not going to believe this, Colonel," explained Dangermouse, "but along comes

this weird cowboy and rescues us!"

"What about the buildings?" asked the Colonel.

"Oh, they're all back where they should be, Colonel," replied Dangermouse cheerfully.

"And Greenback?"

"In jail, sir!"

"So everything worked out all right then?" said the Colonel with relief.

"Well, not quite, sir," said Penfold nervously.

"You see, sir," said Dangermouse, "we solved one problem, but we seem to have brought another back with us!"

As he spoke, a hail of arrows whistled through the slit in the pillar box and thudded into the wall above Dangermouse's head.

"Perhaps you'd better sound the Last Post, eh, DM?" chuckled the Colonel.

The RETURN of COUNT DUCKULA

In the secret Baker Street headquarters of the world's most intrepid hero, Penfold was engrossed in a book on vampires. A hand descended lightly on his shoulder and he shot up in terror.

"Waaagh!" he screamed. "You can't have my blood!"

"Blood, Penfold?" said Dangermouse in surprise. "I was thinking more of China tea and a soft-boiled egg!"

"Oh, it's *you*, chief!" gasped Penfold with relief. "I'll see to it right away."

As he disappeared towards the kitchen, the videophone rang and Colonel K came on.

"Ah, Dangermouse," he said. "Thank goodness you're there!"

"Hello, Colonel," said Dangermouse. "What's the problem?"

"The problem, DM," continued the Colonel, "is the dreaded Count Duckula!"

"Good grief, sir!" cried Dangermouse. "Not the Transylvanian Vampire Duck? I haven't heard anything of him since I was after two of his feathers!"

"Feathers, DM?" said the Colonel blankly.

"Yes, sir, you remember. They were part of a secret formula to save Penfold's life. He nearly drove me crackers! He was showbiz mad!"

"Not was — *is*!" said the Colonel gravely. "And he's threatening to turn the whole government showbiz mad too, unless . . ."

"Unless what, sir?" interrupted Dangermouse.

"It's grim news, DM — unless he gets his own TV show!"

"Good grief!" cried Dangermouse. "He's absolutely terrible! If he gets it, he'll ruin the

industry!''

''And if he doesn't,'' warned the Colonel, ''he'll ruin the country! How do you fancy a Cabinet full of comedians?''

''Well, it wouldn't be as bad as a sideboard full of singers, sir!''

''This is no time for jokes, DM!'' snapped the Colonel. ''Heavens' man, there'll be fifty million performers and no audience before he's through. It'll be the end of entertainment!''

''Don't worry, sir,'' said Dangermouse confidently. ''Penfold and I will sort it out!''

The videoscreen went blank, leaving Dangermouse to ponder on the problem.

''Now, where do I find Count Duckula?'' he mused. ''Bavaria? Bermuda? Bognor? Or maybe . . .''

''Behind you?'' suggested a voice.

With a puff of smoke and a theatrical flourish, Count Duckula himself appeared.

''See where he comes, my friend!'' he cried. ''Have I got plans for you! We're going to be 'Duckula and Dangermouse' — the double act of the decade! But first I've got to 'convert' you!'' He advanced threateningly on Dangermouse and gave a mad laugh.

Suddenly Penfold emerged from the kitchen carrying an egg from which green smoke was drifting.

"Looks like we've got another bad egg here, chief," he said.

"Aaagh! No! A bad egg!" screamed Duckula. "Avaunt!" With that, he disappeared as quickly as he had come.

"Penfold, you've done it!" cried Dangermouse.

"Not yet, sir," replied his puzzled assistant. "But the tea's brewed."

"No, Penfold, the bad egg!" continued Dangermouse. "You've found the ultimate weapon against the vampire duck!"

"But my book says that vampires hate garlic!"

"With Duckula it must be bad eggs! You're a hero! Come on!"

Within seconds, our heroes were racing through the city in search of their foe. Colonel K suddenly appeared on the car's videoscreen.

"Ah, there you are, DM," he cried. "Blighter's struck again! There's a couple of busloads of idiots all demanding parts with the Royal Shakespeare Company!"

"Good grief!" exclaimed Dangermouse. "Then we'd better find him quickly!"

"One of our chaps reported seeing a nasty-looking duck popping in to a theatre in Dreary Lane," added the Colonel.

"Dreary Lane, eh?" mused Dangermouse. "I suspect, sir, that he's hiding out in the tunnels under London's theatre-land. We'll look into it right away!"

So it was that Dangermouse and

a distinctly timorous Penfold found themselves in a deserted street outside the Dreary Lane Theatre.

"Cor, chief," said Penfold nervously. "I don't like the sound of all this silence!"

"Don't worry," Dangermouse reassured him. "It's daytime and everyone knows that vampires sleep through the day — they only come out at night."

"Then we're safe, chief?"

"Of course. Vampires can't stand the sun — they just frazzle up!"

"Then what's *he* doing over there?" said Penfold uneasily, pointing over Dangermouse's shoulder.

Lying on a sun-lounger in the shade of a high wall was Duckula, wearing sunglasses and an old-fashioned striped bathing costume.

"Just a minute!" cried Dangermouse. "This isn't right. Everyone knows that the sun burns vampires to a frazzle! It's just as well you're in the shade."

"Absolute rubbish, Cyril!" scoffed Duckula. "Where did you hear that?"

"It's a fact!" persisted Dangermouse. "Everybody knows it — and don't call me Cyril!"

"OK, smarty-pants!" sneered Duckula. "Watch this!"

He leapt off the sun-lounger into the sunshine and with a wild yell was burnt to a frazzle.

"Aaargh!" he shrieked. "If there's one thing I can't stand, it's a know-it-all!"

He advanced threateningly on our two heroes, but they suddenly

held up bad eggs in front of him.

"Hold it right there, Duckula!" cried Dangermouse, "or it's bad eggs for you! One whiff and you're a goner — so you'd better come quietly!"

"Quietly?" snarled Duckula defiantly. "Never!" He took a clothes peg from inside his cloak and clamped it over his beak.

"The devil!" muttered Dangermouse. "He's got an anti-rotten-egg-peg! Penfold, I think we'd better . . ."

With a fearsome cry, Duckula leapt on the hapless pair and a tremendous fight ensued. When the dust finally settled,

Dangermouse and Penfold were left juggling and cartwheeling — transformed by Duckula's spell.

"Quick, Penfold," gasped Dangermouse. "Throw me that bad egg!"

"Crumbs, chief," said Penfold. "But you're keeping seven up already!"

"Not to juggle with!" cried Dangermouse desperately. "And anyway, these are balls, not eggs."

"Sorry, chief, but I don't seem able to reach my pockets!"

"Pity. I reckon the smell would cure us! Hang on though — there may be something in that dustbin."

Dangermouse crashed into it and came up brandishing a rotten cabbage.

"We're saved, Penfold!" he cried triumphantly. "This works as well! Here, catch!"

"Urgh! Thanks, chief!" muttered Penfold dubiously, as the cabbage hit him full in the face.

"Right, let's go!" said Dangermouse, reverting to his normal self.

"Great idea, chief. I could murder a cup of tea!"

"Not *home*, Penfold! After that villain! We're going to stop Duckula if it's the last thing we do!"

They stumbled along in the dark for a while until Penfold tripped over something lying on the floor.

"Good grief!" exclaimed Dangermouse, picking it up. "A cricket bat! I used to be in the first eleven, you know!"

With a puff of smoke, the bat turned into Count Duckula.

"That's a cracker!" Duckula chuckled. "Vampire *bat*! D'you get it, eh?"

"Oh, that's an awful joke!"

protested Penfold.

"Awful?" cried Duckula. "Knockest thou my gags, varlet?"

He advanced menacingly on Penfold, but Dangermouse sprang between them holding the cabbage.

"Back, you evil wretch!" he cried.

"Aargh, no! Not that!" screamed Duckula. "Not rotten cabbage! I am dying!"

Overacting terribly, he fell to the floor, writhing and twitching.

"By Jove, Penfold!" whispered Dangermouse. "I think we've done it!"

Duckula sat up suddenly with an evil grin.

"Good, wasn't I?" he cackled. "Now, my interfering friend, watch how you go!"

He pressed a button and Dangermouse fell through the floor into a dismal cell below. Metal bands shot out of the wall and bound him fast.

"Now," snarled Duckula, advancing on Penfold. "Let me give you a sneak preview of my hypnotist's act, laddie! You'll love it!"

He held his fingers out in front of Penfold's eyes and began to speak in a soft, soothing voice.

"You are falling into a deep, deep sleep."

"No I'm not!" said Penfold crossly.

"Yes you are!"

"I tell you, I'm not!"

Duckula looked at his fingers suspiciously.

"That's funny!" he muttered. "They were working this morning!"

Suddenly a burst of hypnotic force shot out of the ends. His eyes went glassy and he staggered backwards through the trap-door.

"Good grief!" cried the muffled voice of Dangermouse. "Will you stop throwing vampire ducks at me and get me out of here?"

"Do I have to, chief?" whined Penfold nervously.

"Yes!" cried Dangermouse impatiently. "But watch out for the booby-traps!"

"The what, chief?"

"The booby-traps!" cried Dangermouse desperately.

Steel bands suddenly shot out and pinned Penfold to the wall.

"Waaagh, booby-traps!" he wailed. "You might have warned me!"

"Aha!" gloated Duckula, emerging from the shadows. "A booby trapped! I have you both caught at last! Now I have an audience. So — on with the show!"

Dangermouse and Penfold found themselves bound to seats in a huge theatre. A pair of curtains opened and Duckula appeared in a bathing costume on a high diving board.

"Ladies and gentlemen!" he announced. "The stupendous Count Duckula — high diver extraordinaire — will now attempt the most amazing act of aquatic acrobatic diving! Six hundred feet into a thimbleful of water!"

With a loud drum-roll, he dived headfirst into the thimble and came up splashing and spluttering.

"Aaargh! I've just remembered I can't swim!" he cried. "Curtain!"

When they reopened, an ornate sign read: *'Count Duckula, the knife-throwing miracle, with his assistant, the Phantom of the Panto!'* Duckula bounded on to the stage with a fistful of knives and flung them towards the

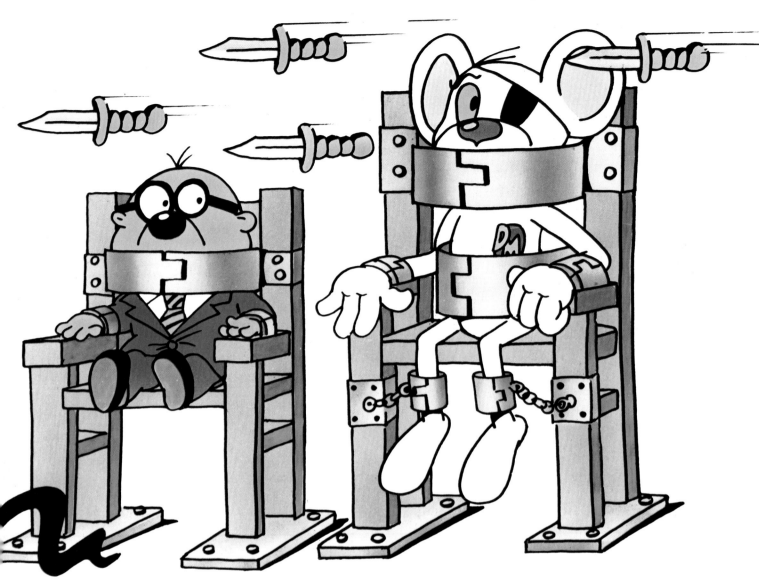

Phantom, who stood in front of a large target. When he had finished, the Phantom looked rather like a pin-cushion.

"Er, let's not be hasty," stammered Duckula nervously. "It was an accident, honestly!"

With an angry roar, the Phantom plucked out the knives and hurled them back at Duckula, who rushed off the stage with a cry of terror.

A succession of dreadful acts followed — *Duckula and Gertie, the one and only stilt-walking elephant, Count Duckula, the feathered cannonball,* and *Herb Duckula and his Transylvanian Brass.* The sight of Duckula in a Hawaian silk shirt, playing a trumpet, was too much for our long-suffering heroes.

"I'm sorry, Penfold!" cried Dangermouse. "I can't take any more of this!"

"Me neither, chief!"

With frantic shrieks, they burst their bonds and raced for the exit.

"Wonderful, wonderful!" exclaimed Duckula. "Delirious with joy! Overwhelmed by my performance! Now I know I'm ready for the big time!"

"Crikey, chief!" said Penfold, as they stood gasping outside in the street. "Whatever shall we do?"

"I don't know!" admitted Dangermouse. "I couldn't have taken another act! Maybe he'll stay down there."

"No, chief, look!" said Penfold miserably.

"Good grief, it's *him*!" cried Dangermouse in despair. "He's trying to talk people into asking for his autograph!"

"He's coming this way!" wailed Penfold.

"Don't worry, I'm ready for him!" said Dangermouse bravely. He leapt on Duckula, threw a sack over his head, bound him tightly with ropes and chains, and padlocked him in a huge crate labelled — TO AUSTRALIA. A large crane drove up, picked up the crate and drove off again.

"Fixed him!" cried Dangermouse with relief. "Come on, Penfold, we're going home!"

They were sitting happily in their car, when a familiar voice began.

"There was a young lady from Ealing. . ."

"Come on, Penfold," said Dangermouse. "I know it's all over, but there's no need to be silly!"

"But I never said a word, chief!" protested Penfold.

"Well someone did!" said Dangermouse suspiciously. He slammed on the brakes and got out of the car. Duckula's head appeared over the back seat.

"Greetings, my friends!" he grinned, putting his arms round them. "Why not let me join you? There — 'tis done!"

He rushed off with a mad laugh, leaving our heroes stitched together.

"Good grief!" muttered Dangermouse. "He *has* joined us — together! Right, that does it!" He ripped at the stitches.

They chased after Duckula and managed to corner him, but he immediately went into a dreadful sob-story.

"Look not so fierce upon me!" he wailed. "'Tis but a little thing I crave — a TV show, no more! I am no villain, but a poor lonely orphan duck, cast out upon the cruel world . . ."

"I can't stand much more of this!" said Dangermouse.

"It's sad, isn't it?" sniffed Duckula miserably.

"It isn't sad," said Dangermouse. "It's awful! It's the worst performance I've ever seen in my life!"

At that moment, a tiny stranger in a large stetson walked in.

"Hey there, ma fine feathered friend," he drawled. "Do that again!"

"What?" cried Duckula, hardly able to believe his ears. "Didst request an encore?"

"Nope, I did not! I just want ya to do it again."

"Your wish is my command!" beamed Duckula, and he began the whole dreadful routine again.

"Yup, I was right," said the stranger when Duckula had finished. "That's the worst performance I ever did see! I'm a big-time US showbiz agent, and

I'm-a signin' you up!"

"Showbiz? The States?" cried Duckula in amazement. "I've made it! I've hit the big-time!"

He leapt into a huge cadillac with the stranger and the car roared away . . .

So, as Duckula swept America and Penfold dusted the sideboard, Dangermouse reported the strange tale to Colonel K.

". . . and then this odd sort of a chap in a stetson whisked him off to America, sir. I can't *think* what for!"

"For life, I hope!" muttered Penfold.

"Well, we've had a report from our man in Washington," said Colonel K. "Seems Duckula's taking the place by storm. Hollywood's at his feet, Broadway's watching his every move!"

"Good grief, sir!" exclaimed Dangermouse. "He must be driving the Americans batty!"

"Worse than that!" continued the Colonel. "They reckon he's so bad, that one performance and you know exactly what *not* to do! He's opening his own acting academy! Making a fortune!"

"That's it then, chief!" chuckled Penfold. "I'm going to retire from all this and run a school for cowards."

COLONEL 'K'